The
Afternoon

To Sue,

Enjoy the book

Elaine Colton

Also by Elaine Colton

The Newport Girls

The *Afternoon*

Elaine Colton

To order additional copies of this book, contact:
Xlibris Corporation
1-888-795-4274
www.Xlibris.com
Orders@Xlibris.com
133453

Contents

For Rick, the one and only true love of my life

Acknowledgments

This book is a work of fiction. Some aspects of the story are based on true events, but all characters are fictitious.

As with any book, it "takes a village." Mine was small, but very useful. A huge thank-you to Mary Anne Ciriello, who read the first draft; Mo Sykes, whose comments added richness to the story, and my partner for life, Rick Leeds, whose valuable point of view, suggestions, editing, and formatting were a gift.

The Journey Begins

The cab pulled up in front of the bar. It had been thirty years since Jo had been here, and there was something very deep inside that evoked some powerful memories about going back into her past. It had been a very important part of her social scene in her early middle life—when she felt that she was hot. Jo was on a journey to relive the parts of her life that had brought her such pleasure and, once, great pain. She was going to revisit every man in her life who had helped shape her, or had she already been shaped when they showed up? *Interesting*, she thought. Maybe it made no difference. Either way, she was going on that journey.

The streets and the building were the same. The only difference was the name on the building's front entrance. Everything else looked exactly the way it had the last time she had been there. Now it was called THE CLUB written in very small, elegant letters on the side of the door, giving off an air of sophistication. It had been the place to be seen back then, and she always felt special, being let in by a huge bouncer in a custom-made suit, who decided whether you belonged or not before he let you in. This decision-making process took place inside the door—another sign of sophistication. It was almost funny that she even remembered the street it was on, but so many of her memories were formed in this place . . . and about the rest of her life as well.

It's very hard to go back thirty years and rely on your memory: some of the experiences that make a woman sensual in her adulthood may be difficult to revisit, but Jo was going to try it anyway. It seemed to be in her destiny, and it just seemed the right time to do it anyway. She needed to know that, at almost age seventy, she still had *it*!

It really wasn't about sex, even though she had experienced a great deal of that during these times in her life: it was about all the recollections and everything that had gone on in the last thirty years. She took a seat at the bar all the way at the end, just where she sat many years before. It was a Sunday afternoon, and there were hardly any people in there, but her thoughts drifted to those splendid weekday evenings when excitement abounded and sex was in the air. The fact was sex began here. It was a non-spoken event. But what she remembered the most about those awesome evenings in her late thirties was the excitement of the chase, the game, and her own sensuality . . . and what it was like to have a man come on to her even if nothing was to happen out of it.

She never was a big drinker, so one drink was all she needed or wanted. If she got the right spot at the bar where she was visible—and she always found the right spot at the bar to be visible—somewhere during the evening, some man, for the most part a gentleman, because that's all who frequented this club, would approach her to dance, to flirt, to have idle chitchat, and sometimes to even have a drink. Jo recalled she had the most amazing experience there one Sunday afternoon, and she fondly remembered the entire event. She can't remember what year, but it still put a smile on her face. She'd been going with the Bulgarian, a charming breed of man: very seductive, elusive, sexy, and dark. Her relationship with him was fabulous until one day . . . he just dumped her. And that was that—the Bulgarian was gone . . . out of her life. She was furious. Nothing had gone wrong; she'd done nothing, but he had just moved on, as most men did. What came next was what put the smile on her face. It took Jo a while to get over him; she just chalked it up to Eastern European men being too into themselves.

One afternoon, shortly after the Bulgarian had run out of her life, Jo went to the movies with her friend, a very interesting woman of German descent, Gerta, who was much older than she and far more experienced in the ways of the world. Sometime during the movie, Jo decided that she wanted to go back to The Club, even though it was Sunday afternoon. She wanted to pick up the first man who walked through the door, take him to his place, and screw his brains out. Then she just wanted to leave him, just like men did to women.

Jo wanted to know what it was like to be a seductress and then discard her conquest like some piece of meat. In retrospect, it was rather devious, but in reality, it was very exciting. After the movies, she and Gerta drove up to The Club and parked. It was always easy to find a parking space on a Sunday afternoon, and they went into the empty establishment and sat down for a glass of wine. It was early evening, and they were the only patrons in the bar at that time. She felt like a lioness waiting for her next meal. The first man who walked through that door was her prey, and he didn't know it.

While Jo and Gerta waited, they laughed about what was about to happen. Jo wondered if this was what men did before they tried seducing a woman. It was sort of exciting lying in wait, not knowing whom the victim would be and praying it was someone somewhat attractive and charming and vulnerable and sexy.

As time passed and no one appeared, Jo decided to give up on this quest. It didn't matter since she and Gerta were laughing so hard from the thought of it anyway. As they were about to leave, the door opened, and in he walked, just an ordinary-looking guy in a trench coat. It seemed quite silly, but she was going to play the game anyway. The bar set the mood: a smooth beat by Frank Sinatra was playing in the background, the lights were turned down low; it was very enticing, and she decided to make her move. Jo sauntered toward her prey and started a trivial conversation, the way most men had always started conversations with her.

"Hello, handsome. What brings you here on this lovely Sunday afternoon? May I sit down and join you for a drink?" He seemed flattered, whoever he was, and she joined him. Gerta watched at the other end of the bar and could hardly contain herself at what was going on before her eyes. Jo and Gerta had made an agreement that Gerta would take the car home because Jo was going to have her way with this man no matter what and would be on her own. Finding a way home before work on Monday was hardly a problem for her; she was hot, and it looked like this guy would do just fine.

Things went quite well, actually. He did all the right things: bought her a drink, danced a little, and flattered her in all the right ways. After a few hours of playful chitchat, Jo went in for the kill.

"I want to fuck you," she finally said.

He almost fainted—but being *a man*, being led by his penis, he said simply, "OK, come with me. I'm staying at the Plaza." Jo went for her coat, signaling for Gerta that everything was going well and she could leave. Jo was now on her own and would play it out, whatever happened.

When they arrived at his hotel room, all hell broke loose. They were barely inside the door when clothes started flying all over the place, and they dove into the bed, kissing each other passionately all over.

Jo took command right away (after all, this was *her* fantasy), and they spent hours satiated by each other's warm bodies. She couldn't remember even stopping to eat or use his bathroom, but they fucked till they dropped. At some point in this seduction, when they came up for air, Jo told this guy why she had picked him up in the first place. She didn't want anything from him but pure, unadulterated sex. He was happy to oblige. After a moment of acknowledgment, they resumed right where they'd left off. They never really talked with each other after that, neither really wanting idle chatter to get in the way of the raw sex they were experiencing. At some point in the very dark of the night, they eventually both collapsed.

Thank goodness for her internal clock. It woke Jo at around 5:00 a.m., allowing her to get her clothes on, get out the door, find a cab, get home, take a shower, get dressed, and get to work on time. Needless to say, as she remembered, she had a very good day—even though somewhat exhausted.

They had never even known each other's name. It was fabulous! One of those *great* life experiences that she has never regretted.

That was the beginning of her sexual awakening. Although she'd had several encounters with men during and after her marriage, she felt this experience was sort of a coming of age. She was forty years old, and it was a new frontier for her. It brought back so many thoughts that were hard to absorb over one drink, and since she really wasn't a drinker, Jo would have to find another way to process these memories. After all, it wasn't the past that haunted her or what she wanted to celebrate: it was today—the now—the life she had today. Jo was a woman who truly lived in the *now*.

Before she came to New York on her very first day of therapy, which she embarked upon after her marriage ended (because of her perceived lack of self-esteem), her therapist said she wanted to deal with issues from Jo's earlier life. Jo said no: she only wanted to deal with the here and now.

The therapist had a deep, brooding look on her face and suggested to Jo that perhaps she'd like to find another doctor because she wasn't sure if she and Jo could make any progress with Jo's attitude. Jo liked this woman (she was kind of a throwback to hippiedom) and suggested they give it a try and see how things turned out. They both finally agreed, and Jo felt that, over the years, as they stayed connected with each other, they had learned so much from their give-and-take. Relationships have a better possibility of working out when both minds are open, so Jo always was to believe.

Around the same time Jo experienced the "Sunday man" from The Club, Jo had moved in with Gerta and was very grateful to have a single friend when her apartment went on the market. It was a condo, and she had been an ideal tenant, but the owners wanted to sell, and Jo didn't have the money to buy it at the time, so you get the unhappy ending here. Gerta had an extra bedroom, and Jo was happy to pay half the rent. For several years, Jo and Gerta played hard in the city, so to speak. For some reason, Gerta didn't have to work. Jo just assumed Gerta was rich, and their money was never discussed. Jo worked hard but very close to where they both lived, so they could party as much as they wanted. Jo's main business was in Manhattan, and it was an easy cab ride for Gerta to get to the city and meet Jo after work.

No question, Jo was the baby in this partnership. Gerta knew of all the hot spots for the over-forty crowd, and Jo just tagged along.

That's how Jo discovered The Club (who knows what it was called back then). Gerta was a pro when it came to attracting men; she was a "male magnet," as Jo remembered. Her gorgeous blonde hair and German accent didn't hurt either. Jo and Gerta would be regulars at least twice a week at The Club and, on the other nights, hit another club on the other side of town. It was here where Gerta introduced her to the Bulgarians, a memorable experience, although it didn't quite work out so well for Jo.

To this day, Jo has no idea how Gerta knew them in the first place. But that was part of Gerta's mystique; she knew these Eastern Europeans: polished, debonair, distinguished, and a throwback to an earlier time of real gentlemen. It was exciting to be let into this circle. They never did drugs, to Jo's knowledge, but they smoked like chimneys, a small price to put up with. Jo felt special, like she was inside some inner circle or something.

Jo only saw one Bulgarian, but one was enough for her. He would always wine and dine her, exuding romance and charm that would make any woman jealous with envy. But then he *always* wanted to have sex too. It was glorious. Jo was just beginning menopause and, for that matter, was very hot herself. It was grand to have a man who wanted her all the time. She grimaced to herself as she sat at the end of the bar, reliving those memories, still asking herself how he could just leave her so abruptly . . . *Funny,* she thought, *I can remember so much of that time and yet can hardly remember what I did two days ago.*

As time passed, Jo and Gerta eventually parted ways. Gerta drank way too much and smoked incessantly. Once, when Jo hosted a party for some friends, Gerta decided to climb onto Jo's desk and dance the night away. It was so mortifying. Secretly, Jo wished she could have been as free as Gerta, but her inhibitions got in the way (she was very hot on the outside but, deep down, very shy inside). When Jo had met Gerta, she was instantly intrigued as to who this woman was. Jo was amazed when Gerta wanted to befriend her; they were so different in every way imaginable. Jo never thought of herself as a cultured woman. Gerta seemed to have come out of the womb in the know.

Gerta had a thing for a professor at NYU. How their paths crossed, Jo was mystified, but one thing she did know: this guy was not going to give up his stature or position in life for a drunk like Gerta. Gerta always lived on the edge, and one never knew what she'd do after a few drinks. Often, Jo stayed home while Gerta went out to play and, when she returned, would throw herself on Jo's bed. It was very uncomfortable for Jo. On her nights at home, after a while, Jo would lock her bedroom door. She didn't know if Gerta was bisexual, but she was *not* going to find out.

Jo smiled slightly with that thought as she sipped her wine at the bar. That had been a pretty wild time in her life. She decided to try and conjure up other "men memories" from her past. Some came flooding into the moment, and she had to stop and catch her breath. There were so many. Had she been a man, she (he) would have been called a player, but as a woman, she'd have been called a slut . . . or worse. After all, some of the men in her life she really had seduced, and she couldn't deny the fact that she had been a part of several one-night stands. Some men she seduced had been married, some she had fallen madly in love with. She felt like Lady Chatterley; time for a break in this quest to see if it was all over at nearly seventy.

She left her wine on the bar and asked the bartender if he'd hold her seat and drink while she walked around the block. He said it was fine, as it was a quiet afternoon with very few patrons. Jo grabbed her coat, and as she headed for the door, she stopped to hear Frank sing a few more words from "All the Way." It was always one of her favorites.

The cold, afternoon New York air caught her by surprise. Why, she couldn't say. After all, she'd lived in the area for over thirty years, and it hardly should have been a shock. Jo really began to reflect as she walked the cold, long blocks of the city.

She had grown up in Le Claire, Iowa. At the time she lived there, it was a relatively small town with just over three thousand people.

Jo had lived a very comfortable life as a single child. Her parents were together until the day they died. Her mother was a stay-at-home mom (hardly any married women with children worked sixty-odd years ago). Her father was a family-practice doctor, and for Iowa standards, they were pretty well off.

She lived a fairly simple, happy childhood as an only child. Jo found out, many years later, her mother had complications during childbirth and was unable to have any more children. Jo had been a 4-H'er, joined a lot of clubs in high school, and even got into Iowa State University, determined to have a college education. She felt strongly that she might need these credentials someday, and of course, she was right.

It was in college that she met her future husband, a great guy from Des Moines studying journalism, hoping to become a writer on *The Des Moines Register*. His name was Jeffrey, and her family liked him very much. Jeff got the job he had wanted after graduation and asked Jo to move with him to Des Moines. She would have no part of it without a formal commitment. He proposed, wanting to marry her anyway. With joy, she accepted. Little did Jo know at that time that life with Jeff would not all be a bed of roses.

It took her years to leave the marriage. As she began her life with Jeff, she could vividly recall his demands from the beginning of their relationship. She had never seen any of this when they were in college. He demanded sex at the drop of a hat and was appalled that she could never completely satisfy him. *Huh,* Jo thought, *it never occurred to him to please me.* Thank goodness there were no children born of this marriage, and thank goodness Jo had a very good job as a sales associate at a major department store in Des Moines. She was planning a career in merchandising, and she felt very lucky to have her job to take her mind off Jeff. No one in her family had ever been divorced, and she felt very stuck.

Her boss was a charming, married executive and took an immediate liking to Jo. She was flattered and delighted to join him for lunch every now and then. These luncheons led to more romantic adventures after work, and since Jeff was out often covering stories, her absence wasn't even an issue.

Jo realized going to a motel out of town was not appropriate and hardly romantic, but when she got in bed with this man, another world opened up to her. She discovered her own fire and was enthralled with lovemaking that actually included her. This went on for years until she knew she had to put a stop to it all. Jeff was oblivious to it all but accepted a divorce nonetheless. He really had not been happy in their marriage; according to him, he felt "stuck as well." He had no idea that Jo was having a torrid affair—two, actually—so he was totally relieved when she declared her wishes to end their loveless marriage.

As she remembered his domineering ways, she reinforced, in her mind, that no man would dominate her again. When she ended her marriage, the reason was irreconcilable differences. She certainly held to that, as she never married again.

She really had no experience when it came to sex prior to her marriage. In high school, she remembered going behind the school building one night with a boyfriend and rubbing against his body. Her surprise was almost ridiculous when he started to get hard. She honestly didn't know what that meant. She knew kissing felt good, but anything else was totally foreign to her.

Going back to her marriage, her husband was very disappointed at her lack of attention, and even though he made sure that he was satisfied, Jeff never gave it a second thought to give her pleasure as well. During this prolonged marriage, Jo had begun not one but two affairs with married men. The second affair was even more exciting than with her boss; this man thought she was the hottest thing he had ever seen. It was like a true validation that she was not the cold fish her husband said she was. Not long after the affair began, Jo realized she really didn't want to live a double life, so she ended both the affair and her marriage.

These remembrances came through like the floodgates of her soul had been opened.

Both bold moves for her, she decided to take one more. So Jo moved to New York to start life anew, knowing full well she had the goods to be sexual and sensual. Getting a job was not an issue as her parents had connections in New York, and an old friend of her father's decided to take her under his wing; he helped her find a reasonably priced apartment in Queens and introduced her to people who might give her a job.

For many years, as a single woman again, she was free to meet new people and go wherever she wanted. Her job (a sales rep for a large designer and manufacturer of lingerie) put her in contact with a wide array of interesting people, and with her newly found courage, she spread her wings and explored many avenues she would never have had in Iowa. Then along came Sally!

Sally was just as worldly, to some extent, as Gerta was. Not as beautiful but smart as a whip and truly knowledgeable of the New York scene. She and Jo met at a business-networking function and instantly became friends.

Sally, like Jo, had been married once and was far more interested in partying than in finding another husband. Jo was thrilled and happy to follow wherever Sally led. She trusted Sally and sized her up as being a woman in the know, but not one who would bring her into any kind of dangerous situation. And she was right.

The Monday-Night Card Game

Sally told Jo that she knew a very refined group of gentlemen from out of town (Detroit) who came to New York City once every other week on business. They stayed at a very urbane, low-key hotel and always played cards on Monday nights. Sally was heavily involved with one of them, but they were always interested in meeting sophisticated and daring women who would hang around during the game and would be available for dinner and whatever afterward. Sally invited Jo to attend one Monday-night affair, and Jo couldn't resist. It almost felt like something out of *Breakfast at Tiffany's*. She remembered feeling like Holly Golightly: part of something exciting in New York.

Jo became hung up on this wonderful married man by the name of Peter, who was part of the Monday-night card game. It was thrilling to have him respond to her as well. He used to call her Doll, and she loved it. Maybe it was her small-town, unsophisticated ways that attracted him to her, but whatever it was, the sex was hot and fabulous.

This arrangement went on for four years. He would come to town every few weeks to see his large customers. Monday nights were always for the boys and then for her afterward.

Then for the two or three days remaining on his trip, he would wine and dine her at the finest restaurants in New York and then bed her at the Waldorf Astoria. It was a miracle she could get any work of her own accomplished—she was so enthralled with him.

One night, while they were in the theater, watching Lauren Bacall in *Applause, Applause*, he reached over to take Jo's hand during intermission and told her he had a four-carat diamond ring in his vault. She could wear it every time he was in town, he said, and then it would go back in the vault until his next visit. Jo remembered being frozen in time as she realized she was becoming a call girl of some sort. Why wasn't she good enough to wear the ring all the time?

A light bulb went off in her head—*finally*! Was this who she wanted to be? The answer was clearly no, and even though she didn't interrupt the evening by saying so, she knew, in her heart of hearts, this was *not* the kind of life she wanted—notwithstanding a four-carat diamond. The next day, she told Sally she would not be going to any more Monday-night card games. It had been one hell of a ride, but not the ride she wanted. Jo couldn't remember whether she ever told Sally about the ring. She never spoke to the man who called her Doll again either, for that matter.

Her thoughts drifted to two more married men she'd had affairs with after meeting the Monday-night card guys. Sally had a wide array of friends and eventually introduced her to Paul. He was somewhat unique to her. He must have had something very missing from his marriage to want to take up with her, she remembered thinking at the time, but Jo discovered very early on that married men all held a lot of passion. Over time, they probably lost it at home—in their own marriages. Jo laughed, thinking maybe that was why she never married again. Being the other woman had its perks, most definitely.

Jo and Paul went skiing most weekends in the winter (she didn't ski) and boating in the summer. Their times together were only on the weekends, and she once asked him why his wife didn't come along instead of her. He said she really didn't like either activity and was perfectly happy to let him go off with his friends.

Of course, she knew nothing of Jo; for that matter, none of them ever did. *So strange,* she thought. Their lovemaking was spectacular, and Jo was as content as she could ever be.

Then one day, about a year into the affair, Paul came to her and said he wanted to leave his wife to marry her. Jo thought she would have a heart attack on the spot. The current state of their affair was just fine with her; marriage, on the other hand, was a deal breaker. Paul actually cried when she said no, and of course, that was the end of that.

The other man (Lord, she couldn't believe there had been so many) would come to New York on business from time to time. They met at a bar one afternoon when Jo had finished her sales calls early and just stopped in for a quick glass of wine. He was the only other person in the bar at that time and asked if she minded if he joined her. Jo laughed out loud as she remembered using that line herself. His name was Andrew, not Andy. He lived in Chicago, was an attorney for a large law firm, and had clients in New York. That's what brought him to the city.

Well, one thing led to another; after a very expensive meal at Le Cirque, Andrew asked her up to his hotel for a nightcap. *What the heck,* she thought. He's handsome and obviously on a very large expense account, and she was seeing no one at that point in time (like that mattered too much). So she said yes. Thus began the two-year "Chicago to New York" affair. Andrew would call her several days before he came to town, and she'd free her social calendar to be with him. It was perfect until . . . well, until it wasn't anymore. When Jo and Andrew parted ways, she was sure he had already moved onto his next "Jo."

Jo awoke from her vivid memories and suddenly realized how freezing it was on her little walk around the block. She must have walked ten blocks, so she decided to head straight back to the bar. Once perched back on her barstool, she perused the crowd that was now mingling, laughing, and drinking. The bartender saw how cold she was and offered her a cup of coffee on the house. She thanked him and remembered when she had been as young as most of these Gen Xers.

She remembered the man she could never have. She had been in her late forties and had met him through her business. In fact, if memory served her right, all the men she ever met and got involved with (except Mr. Detroit and Peter) were somehow connected through her business.

While Jo was going through her dry period, she got involved with several charities in and around the city. It took her mind off sex and men. It was at this time she bought her first artificial penis.

She had no guidance as to what a good sex toy was, so she took her chances and bought one that looked like it would suffice. Actually, it brought a grin to her face to think of how well it served her between men. About three years went by while she dated off and on, and sex was not as important as it had once been. Jo remembered thinking, *Maybe, after menopause, you don't really want sex anymore.* She knew that wasn't so, though. She was waiting for the right man: he just hadn't shown up yet!

The Right Man That Couldn't Be Hers

It was sometime in the early '90s when this man, Carl, walked into her life. It was a chance meeting at a gallery opening in SoHo. She was a big girl by then and could go by herself, so she did. Carl was not the picture of her dreams, but they started some small talk over hors d'oeuvres. He was gentle, handsome, somewhat overweight, and very interested in what she had to say. This in itself was a total shock to her senses; he was far from a city slicker. After all, most men she'd met over the years were only interested in getting her into bed and themselves.

A friend of hers had once given her a book called *Why Does It Always Have to Be about YOU*, and most of her experience had been with men who were far more interested in themselves, intellectually, than in anything she had to offer—narcissists, to say the least. Carl was perfect in every sense except that he was married. He told her straight up and even showed her a picture of his wife, who was drop-dead gorgeous. Carl said they'd been married over twenty years. Jo couldn't understand what in the world a woman of her caliber could see in him. Although Jo was attractive, she was certainly nowhere in the same league. She asked where his wife was, and Carl said she rarely went out to openings because she found them so inauthentic.

He went to *everything* that was happening in the city every night. Carl never knew whom he was going to meet. It was either a business opportunity or pleasure. Like meeting Jo—that was pleasure. She was flattered.

This guy is really cool and more attractive by the minute, Jo thought. He lived in the city, and she now lived in Brooklyn. Carl said he'd like to see her again perhaps for lunch someday. She couldn't wait to say yes. He mentioned *nothing* about taking her to bed, and she truly loved it. Wow! A real man who was just interested in her. How refreshing and sexy. She thought Carl was younger than she, but she could have cared less. His charm and almost shyness was sexier than anything she'd ever experienced. She was so hot for him she thought she was going to explode, and that was only after an invitation to lunch.

Oh my word, now I can't wait to take him to bed, Jo thought. She chuckled as she remembered a time when all that ever came out of Paris Hilton's mouth was "That's hot." For Jo, this was *hot!*

Everything about him turned her on. His weight was not even an issue. She'd had affairs with two overweight men in the past. As they say, "When you're hot, you're hot. When you're not, you're not." She first heard that in a course she had taken on sex, and she believed it. That's all there was to it. She had to put this experience to bed, once and for all—twenty-five years later. Carl and she saw each other very infrequently, but Jo had made up her mind, at age fifty-something, that she would settle for their relationship just the way it was because he was the perfect man for her. And although he was never going to be hers exclusively, having him every now and then was magic. The funny thing she remembered was, the few times they had made love, it was only so-so. He was not a great lover, but who he was had turned her on so much it didn't matter.

The last time they made love, he was on his way to Boston on business and had her meet him at some motel near LaGuardia. It was hardly the Plaza or the Waldorf from many years before, but it didn't matter; any place with Carl was magic. They quickly undressed and got right down to business. She was on top of him and could have devoured him. Jo was so hot she couldn't contain herself and came so quickly before he was ready it was almost embarrassing. It was a *huge* orgasm, and it startled Carl as much as it did herself. "What the hell was that?" Carl asked.

She'll never forget it till her dying day. "A very big orgasm," she replied.

He was happy and came too. Many years later, Jo learned that you could pee when you're very hot, and as her memory allowed her, she realized that must have been what happened that day. It's a very good thing he took a quick shower before he left for the airport! Jo sat at the bar and laughed out loud. What crazy experiences she had had.

The last time she saw Carl was in her apartment months later, and after their lovemaking, they sat in her small living room and professed their love for each other. This emotional affair had been going on for years. She knew he was never going to leave his gorgeous wife and family, though. By now, he even had a grandson that he was crazy about. Jo gathered her courage about her and said, "Carl, I will be your Katharine Hepburn, and you can be my Spencer Tracy for the rest of my life." Carl looked at her and said with a sad expression on his face, "No." There was a long silence, and Jo knew it was over then. Maybe the love of her life was such a good guy, he wasn't going to have the rest of her life lived this way. He kissed her on the cheek and left. Jo remembered she didn't even cry; she had had something beyond her wildest dreams with Carl and would treasure it until her death.

The next week, he called her to see how she was doing. She told him she was watching an opera on PBS and was quite surprised how moved she was by it. They were singing in Italian and using subtitles on the screen. Jo told him how amazed she was that it didn't get in the way of her powerful emotions. Several days later, in the mail were two tickets to the Met at Lincoln Center. She took a friend. Jo never saw Carl again. He truly was the one and only love of her life—up to that point, that is.

Jo left her thoughts for a moment and checked out the bar scene again. The place was beginning to fill up with the over-forty crowd. Boy, how things had changed; everyone was in jeans or very casual clothes. She must have looked so out of place, all dressed up like the way it had been back then when men were in suits and ladies wouldn't dare arrive if looking less than perfect. There was no question that no one would approach her. She could have been any one of their mothers.

For a moment, a fog of sadness overcame her as she realized she had no children and had made the choice to never remarry. It had its perks though, so she thought, aside from her working responsibilities (and she was so grateful to still be working). She was as free as a bird, had fabulous women friends, and had made enough money over time to do pretty much whatever she felt like doing.

Jo didn't really know if she wanted to continue this journey with herself. It was starting to get heavy. Now she wasn't even sure why she began this Sunday-afternoon adventure in the first place. She asked the bartender if one could still eat at the bar, and he said, "Of course." He brought her a place mat, some water, some silverware, a napkin for her lap, and a menu.

She decided to eat something substantial; after all, she'd been at the bar for hours. She took a break from recalling her past long enough to devour a medium-rare petite filet mignon and salad. She just savored the food as Frank Sinatra crooned to her. Years ago, you could smoke in this joint; now there were No Smoking signs plastered everywhere you ate. She was so grateful for two things at that moment: she'd given up smoking a long time ago, and there was no smoke smell to alter the taste of her delicious steak.

After her meal, Jo conjured up some of the memories of the most powerful man in her life.

The Final Man: The Love of Her Life

It was Curt who had finally swept her off her feet again. Jo was in her late fifties, and Curt was going to truck-driving school to learn how to drive those long-haul rigs cross-country. Apparently, there was very good money in that. Jo had to stretch her memory to remember where in the hell their two paths would have passed. It was crazy as she recalled all the different venues where these men had become part of the fabric of her life. Curt and Jo met at a book signing in the Village. She didn't even know if she liked the author but found it fascinating that an author would sign books and people would stand in line to get their autograph. *What the heck*, she thought at the time. It represented a new adventure she'd never experienced. Well, the writer must have been pretty popular because the line was out the bookstore door and around the corner, but it was summer, so Jo didn't care.

It was in that line that she met Curt, the truck driver in training. Now Jo had to admit she might have been a little bit of a snob, but then again, Curt was laying out $23.95 for a hardcover book and an autograph. There had to be more to him than just being a truck driver, so she struck up a conversation with him. He seemed nice enough and excited about the book.

Actually, he knew a lot about the other books this author had written. She liked that: he was well read; not bad for an almost truck driver. Jo sized him up: a little overweight, very tall, funny, very strong looking, and pleasant. She actually found him somewhat charming. What a real bonus. She thought, *If you have to stand in the line in the heat, far better to have a somewhat-cool adult to speak to than a kid texting with his earplugs in.* Jo turned on her charm and began to enjoy her conversation with Curt. She remembered him telling her he used to sell insurance. With the changing economy, that didn't help him with living expenses, and thus, the truck-driving gig. Jo remembered that she really began to like this guy. Her memory of Curt really started to kick in.

They had their books signed and decided not to go their separate ways just yet. He invited her to have a cup of coffee at a nearby bistro, and she readily accepted his invitation. She didn't know any other way to be, so she acted flirtatious and bold. She really thought she'd always been like this but had to squash that part of her personality when she was growing up in Iowa. Everyone seemed to be very laid-back in her youth, as far as she could recall, but when she got to New York in the '80s, she gave herself permission to break out. She decided that that person was the true Jo.

It served her well for the last thirty or so years. She could let it out in the New York area. She was tame, compared to most folks who lived in New York. It served her well in business. She was fearless, and it certainly didn't hurt with men either. Contrary to popular belief, her experiences had taught her that most men really liked a strong "out there" woman. But there was something about Curt that had her dumb it down a little. She didn't want to be so forward with him; she wanted to sit back, relax, and see if there was anything there besides a really nice man.

The afternoon was turning into twilight at The Club, and even though it was way above her normal self-imposed limit, Jo ordered another glass of wine. She knew she would ultimately take a cab home, so what did it matter anyway? She couldn't turn off the memories. They kept flowing forward.

Back to Curt. He was such a puzzle; they had had such a nice time. It was hard for her to fathom why she hadn't heard from him since they parted. On one level, it made her more interested in him; on the other, she felt a sense of disappointment. Always with a plan B up her sleeve when she was having a lull, Jo would set up dinner and movie dates with her women friends. And most of her spare time outside work was filled with fun things to do. She really had a great life, she thought.

Then the call came, and Jo really had to stifle her excitement. She remembered feeling giddy, like a schoolgirl who was just asked to prom by the high school quarterback. Curt was as matter-of-fact as he could be; there was absolutely no mention of the weeks that had passed since they'd first met. He had been sent to Texas for advanced truck-driving school, and his days and nights had been filled with an inordinate amount of driving, studying, and tests. He hadn't taken her number with him, and the days were too exhausting. He was simply too tired to feel like talking to anyone. He was back in New York now and wanted to see her. At one level, she was quite pleased to learn of such extensive training for truck drivers; on another level, all she wanted to do was be with him. Curt was a little different, though, from most men she'd been with. His first desire wasn't sex; it seemed to genuinely be all about her, or so she thought.

He lived on City Island, a small island on the Bronx end of Long Island Sound. Jo found this fascinating as most of her men had been somewhat more cultured and lived more of a city life. Curt lived on a friend's boat that was docked at one of the many piers on the island. He loved the distinction of going from the quaint, almost New England-like town atmosphere into the action and electricity of the city. Jo was completely fascinated; she couldn't wait to Google *City Island* and learn about it as though it were an exotic island in the middle of the Pacific.

Curt wanted more in the relationship and, in his own bold move, asked if she'd join him for a tour of the island and dinner (or more) on the boat that coming weekend. It was still summer and quite warm, so she accepted. Curt said he'd come and pick her up early Saturday morning. She said it was too far for him to come, and he said something like, "Ma'am, I'm a long-distance truck driver. Driving twenty-three miles is like going to the corner store for a loaf of bread." She laughed at the bar as she remembered his exact words.

That conversation was as fresh in her mind as if it had happened yesterday. And it was many years ago when she and Curt began the love affair of her life. *So funny,* she thought; there were so many that felt like they were the love affair of her life, but Curt—he was different, truly the real deal.

Jo remembered rising each morning with such excitement and counting the days until Saturday morning would arrive. She felt she had to be prepared for anything, so Friday night she had packed a sack pocketbook with extra underwear, a toothbrush, and a hairbrush. She didn't want to mess anything up, and if nothing happened, Curt would be none the wiser, and she wouldn't look foolish. Truth be told, she was not going to take the lead in any way, shape, or form. It was all up to Curt, but she was prepared for the best.

Saturday morning was bright and sunny, and her expectations were brimming. When he arrived, she was almost demure—what had happened to that bold, "out there" woman? Jo consciously put her away and didn't take her out again for a long time until she felt totally safe with Curt. At that time, she didn't know if that was going to happen, but she felt his strength and wanted that to be dominant. He seemed to be as excited as she was when he picked her up on that glorious day—the day they would never forget as long as they lived.

They stopped for coffee and a muffin to go in Brooklyn and laughed, ate, and drank until they entered City Island. The day would end up being one of the most glorious of her life. She really liked Curt; he was truly a man's man yet a charming lady's man as well. What a fabulous combination. Jo was really excited she had gone to that book signing almost a month ago. Fate. You never know who will come into your life, then *bam*! Suddenly, you have an instant connection. She truly was ready to give herself over to him (and perhaps more) that day. She didn't need to run the show at all. It was his show, and she loved it.

The day began with a tour of the island, one of many around the Sound that very few people knew about. City Island was very small and very quaint. There were about six thousand people who lived on the island, and like Curt, many people lived on their boats tied up at the many docks and marinas around the yacht club. He delighted in showing her everything; it seemed to be his own special world, far away from driving a truck. She loved being led and thoroughly enjoyed his joy.

She had never met anyone like Curt, and her memory of him was as vivid as if they'd seen each other yesterday. They strolled the streets hand in hand, like lovers in waiting. She felt a blush come upon her and was embarrassed. After all, Jo was close to sixty and had no idea she was capable of that kind of girlish feeling. Jo recalled his looking down at her and smiling at her genuine discomfort. He had actually liked it. They stopped for lunch near one of the piers and devoured oysters, clam cakes, and wine. They laughed silently at the anticipation of what might await them. After lunch, Curt finally drove to the dock where his friend's boat was tied up, and they walked down to the slip.

Jo was surprised at how big it was, and once again, Curt explained how he was fortunate enough to live there. Curt's friend traveled all over the world and had a magnificent apartment in the city. He was gone more than he was home and was glad to have Curt watch the boat when he was away, just like house sitting. Then, pretty soon, Curt would be on the road, maybe for weeks at a time, and would lock the boat up until he returned. The dock master, who was a very good friend of the owner, would keep an eye on it.

Jo thought this sounded like a very vagabond way to live, but it truly had an air of thrill attached to it. Besides boat sitting, Curt knew how to maneuver the boat out into the Sound and, having asked Jo to bring a sweater and scarf with her, asked if she'd like to take a cruise. *Yes* was the only answer, and she helped him untie the ropes as they slowly left the dock. On a very low throttle, the two headed out to Long Island Sound.

Curt was masterful. He definitely knew his way around boats. Jo sat on a seat nearby, and after a few moments, Curt asked if she'd like to take the wheel. She said yes and was pleased to have this latest experience. He came up behind her and put his hands on hers to help her steer. She remembered him leaning into her and rubbing up against her butt. He was aroused, and so was she. He suggested they stop and anchor right then, and after he was sure that the anchor was secure, he gently pulled her to him and kissed her with more passion than she'd ever had in her life.

She melted in his arms and collapsed to the sheer ecstasy. He literally took her breath away for several moments. Quietly they went below, and without a word, he slowly undressed her and then himself. *This is crazy,* she thought. They had fifty-something-year-old bodies, but she didn't care. He was gorgeous. They were still standing, not on the bed yet, and he put his hands on her breasts. She thought she was going to pass out from the heat—the heat coming off her body. He couldn't stop kissing her; her tongue was halfway down his throat.

It was like a scene out of a foreign film. *If I died on the spot, what a way to go,* Jo thought. It was beyond anything she had ever felt before. She knew about lust and hotness but every other experience she had had paled in comparison to this. Curt gently moved her to the double bed at the bow of the boat.

Not a word was spoken. She vividly remembered that they had said nothing. His hands were all over her body, and her passion led her to reciprocate. He was so big and strong and sweaty she thought she was going to pass out from the ecstasy of it all. She let out a groan as his hand slid between her legs. She welcomed him in and found the parts of him that were going to be intertwined with her shortly. He let out a manly sigh, and it was clear that they were both in the pleasure of the experience. He was very soft with her, as hard as he was. It was clear he wanted to gratify her first before himself.

Their lovemaking seemed to go on forever in Jo's memory, and she screamed and bent her body into his as she had her first orgasm. He smiled and kissed her over and over. She thought she would pass out from the passion. He must have come several more times before he let himself go. The sheets were so wet they felt like they were melting into a sea of sex. They lay very quietly, and he stroked her breasts again as he kissed her tenderly. When they both came up for air, they just stayed silent in bed. They held hands and looked at each other, somewhat in disbelief. Here they were, middle-aged and completely in heat as if they'd been in their twenties. They both smiled and then broke out into huge laughter, hugging each other very closely under the sweaty, wet sheets.

Exhausted, both of them fell asleep for a bit, and when they awoke, they decided, consciously, that they couldn't go through that again. Jo remembered thinking, *Can I even get out of bed and walk?* Let alone on a boat swaying and rocking in the water. Finally, they both decided they'd give it a try. As they got up slowly, they stripped the sheets and put them in a bag for Curt's laundry. The size of the shower was barely big enough for Curt. They both decided to squeeze in together, and the shower became the next sexual encounter.

He lathered up his hands and caressed her breasts until her nipples felt like they'd doubled in size. She was crazed once again. She reciprocated her lust to all his private parts, and his heat returned once again. He glided his cock into her as smoothly as a seal slides into the ocean. Jo thought she had completely lost her mind.

Somehow they were able to finish their shower and dry each other off between passionate kisses. They then dressed, half in awe of what had just taken place. Neither of them could really comprehend the magnitude of what had just occurred. It was so beyond lust. It felt more like new love even though they both realized that seemed preposterous. As they dressed and thought of it all, the need for food also came into their consciousness. They realized they hadn't eaten anything but each other since lunch yesterday and were starved; thank goodness they were not out in the Sound too far. It would take just a short trip to pull up at a dock and find a down-home cookery. Curt took the wheel and high-throttled the engine to get them to port ASAP. Jo remembered that she put her arms around his waist and leaned into him with her head the whole way there. She couldn't remember being so happy but was almost afraid this was somewhat of a fantasy.

Devouring breakfast, they quietly relived the last twenty-four hours together. Neither of them was glib about anything. Jo thought they both were overwhelmed by their unbridled passion that had swept them away. On the way back to Brooklyn, they said very little but held hands as a romantic gesture. For whatever reason Jo couldn't remember, they both decided to complete their date that morning and be free to reflect on the entire day before. Jo was OK with that as the experience of their lovemaking had left her somewhat perplexed: was it Curt or her lack of intimacy that had swept her into this state of hotness? She had to sort it out.

By now, Jo had been at the bar for several more hours than she wanted and decided to stop right here—for now. The memories almost led her to tears.

She paid her tab, left the bartender a very big tip, and hailed a cab. Jo headed home for a mindless night of television; she was spent. Tomorrow was another day: a workday, thank goodness, and a break from this drama she had put herself through today.

Happy to be in her safe little haven, Jo got prepared for Monday, watched a little TV as she ate a light dinner, and went to bed. She truly was exhausted.

Monday brought great relief. Back to her routine. The best part of her day was that all the clients she had to see were in the city, and she could be very efficient in getting her obligations met. She loved her clients, and her company so appreciated her they pretty much left her to run her own show. She produced handsomely for them, and they truly stuck by the old adage: "If it ain't broke, don't fix it!"

Jo always had successful sales calls; maybe that's why she'd only worked for two companies over the last thirty years. Her clients loved her, and she felt the same way about them. She'd spent years building the loyalty of her customers, and except for a very few rare screw-ups in an order, her job was less crisis management and more love, nurturing, and expanding her order base.

Jo was glad she had a busy morning that Monday, but her afternoon was light. She wasn't sure, but maybe—just maybe—she'd return to The Club and complete this mental adventure she had chosen to create for herself. The morning went beautifully: happy customers, no screw-ups or complaints, and new orders. She felt very powerful when it came to her ability to please her clients in every professional way, and that was what made her job so gratifying.

Jo had finished her calls by two o'clock, which included lunch with a very good client, and decided to return to The Club. It was open for lunch every day, but the bar was lightly specked with a few men that afternoon, and to her pleasure, when she arrived, a new bartender was on duty and had no idea Jo had spent so many hours there the day before. She ordered a club soda with lime just in case her boss called her back to the office before quitting time.

In Jo's world, it was never quitting time. There were always clients to wine and dine, but she had the choice of when to initiate those evening dinners. Industry meetings were different; they were mandatory. Jo loved to mingle with her clients and the higher-ups she never got to see on a regular call, so that was fun as well. Today she had no obligations; so returning to the bar left her with no unfinished business—professionally, that is.

Her thoughts drifted back to yesterday. She forced herself into a deep-breathing routine so she could explore the situation more fully. Soon the memories came flooding back . . .

There were certain things that were quite evident between Curt and Jo. They certainly shared a sexual, sensual, and passionate connection. *But,* she remembered thinking, *what if that was all there was?* Was that enough? She hadn't had a man in her life since Carl who evoked such feelings.

But Curt is a truck driver. This is insane, she thought. She reflected more on the possibility of falling in love with a truck driver. She remembered being disgusted with herself that she would even think this way. Curt seemed to be a wonderful man and brought her everything sexually that she could ever desire. But she needed to explore his other values and virtues. Her memories were so vivid. It all came rushing back as if it had been yesterday.

In retrospect, Jo was delighted she'd not heard from Curt for several days after their explosive, sexual first date. At the time though, she remembered wondering if she'd ever hear from him again. What if she was just a one-night stand for him? Lord knows she'd had some herself, so who was she to judge? Jo didn't have to wait long for that answer because Curt called soon after and said that he had been reflecting on the very same things she had. She was pleased: it showed that he was a thoughtful man, and she liked that. He was worried that the nature of his career choice might negate the possibilities of a meaningful relationship. After all, as he began this new job, he knew he'd be gone for long periods.

Could a woman like Jo be willing to put up with a relationship like that? When he finally called, he said he'd like to meet her in the city and discuss his thoughts and concerns. Jo invited him to dinner, and he declined, saying he wanted to meet with her in a neutral place where there was no possibility of sex and feeling their newfound attraction would get in the way if they met where there was a chance they'd forget the whole purpose of the date and collapse in each other's arms. That would be the beginning of another night of passion.

He was very quick to say he wanted another night like they'd experienced, just not on this date. She laughed and said she understood and suggested a very reasonable place in the Village. She had a sense that Curt had much less money than she did and didn't want to put him in an awkward situation by picking a fancier restaurant. The place she chose was quiet, and she thought they could have a nice dinner and would be able to talk as well. It was a Monday (how could she remember that?), and they made their date for Wednesday evening. Jo had said she'd meet him there and that she would plan her business day around the city. Curt said his first long haul was not until Saturday and that would be fine.

Jo sat at the bar, reflecting on all the years that were to come with Curt. Her heart almost burst at what was to be.

Wednesday finally came, but suddenly, time had slowed to a standstill. Six o'clock couldn't come soon enough. She had had this feeling only once before—with Carl. Luckily, her preoccupation with work helped to move the day along fairly well, and suddenly, to her delight, it was five thirty—time to hail a cab for the date. When Jo arrived, she had five minutes to spare, but Curt had arrived much earlier than she and was sipping a Stoli on the rocks in anticipation of seeing her.

They practically ran into each other's arms, and their kiss was beyond anything appropriate for a public setting. They caught themselves, unhooked from their embrace, and tried to find a modicum of decorum to continue their evening. As Jo began to sit, Curt pulled out the chair for her, and she thought, *What a gentleman.* She had a feeling she'd be assessing the entire evening and hoped it didn't get in the way of why Curt wanted to see her. This was his show, and she was not going to dominate it in any way and rain on his parade.

After the normal pleasantries, like "How have you been?" and "What's new?" they ordered wine, and Jo started to relax. She loved looking at him. He was not perfectly handsome, but his eyes lit up, and his laugh was large. She found herself appreciating everything about this man whom she had met one afternoon by pure chance. She thought, *Maybe this is how the great loves begin. By chance.* Then she shut her mind off and opened it up to him.

They ordered pasta, and while they waited for dinner to arrive, Curt began to speak. *Amazing,* she thought, *we've almost been having the same thoughts.* It made the hairs stand on the back of her neck. Curt was so excited about his new job opportunity, and when he spoke about it, he was completely unencumbered. Just him. No ties to anyone or anything, and when Jo showed up in his life, for him, it changed the color of everything. Curt went on to share he'd been married twice, but neither wife wanted children. After his last divorce, which was over fifteen years ago, Curt drifted a while, settled on City Island, sold insurance, dated here and there, but never held a commitment to anything romantic with anyone. Jo thought, *we probably would have gone through this on our first date had passion and lust not gotten in the way.*

She smiled as she sat at the bar in The Club. She was so amazed how these memories were so vivid. It had been almost twelve years since that conversation.

Back to their talk. She remembered that she held herself back from saying a word. She didn't want to disrupt his chain of thought. He rambled on some more about being excited about going on the road, and then, she remembered, it came out. Curt said something like (she couldn't recall it word for word), "I never expected to meet a woman like you. You are messing up my life. I had it all planned out. I don't want to lose you. I want to really get to know you. I want you in my life." She held back a sigh.

She didn't want to scare him; men get scared, and she knew there was more to come.

Thank goodness dinner arrived and he took a conversational break. Jo was very careful with her words and asked if he'd mind if she interjected with some thoughts of her own. He said, "By all means." She didn't want to go into the shadier parts of her adulthood. None of that was necessary, as far as she was concerned. That was the past, and Jo only cared about the present.

Jo told Curt she had similar feelings (except for the part about "messing up" her life). She was also amazed at their instant connection and, like him, really wanted to get to know him more deeply. She stopped right there and ate dinner. Again, she didn't want to scare him!

They veered off in a different direction for a while. She asked him about trucking and what that meant for him. She remembered he'd been in Texas to be trained for long hauls. She asked him what that meant. His eyes lit up as he talked about picking up cargo of whatever kind and delivering it to whatever destination it was to go, waiting for more cargo to go who knew where, and ultimately ending up back in New York, his home base. Truckers got paid by the mile and by meeting or exceeding their deadlines. Curt said there was no way of knowing when he'd return until he was assigned a load. He said he could be gone as long as a month or more, and that's what worried him most—that this would force him to lose Jo.

She listened with genuine interest in what Curt had to say. What would it be like to have a man she was truly beginning to have feelings for to be in and out of her life? *Hell*, she thought, *I'd done that with Mr. Detroit and Carl, but this is a far more real situation.* Once again, Jo asked if she could share her thoughts. She remembered how her therapist many years ago had thought they would not work out because it was not the way it was usually done. They ended up having had a perfect partnership. Why couldn't this be the same for her and Curt? It could be a relationship that was just not conventional.

Jo asked Curt if he were daring enough to begin anew with no guarantees of how any of it would work out. Curt looked at Jo with gentle, loving eyes and took her hand. Thus began the almost-ten happiest years of her life. He bent over the pasta plates and gave her a tender kiss. They both had calmed down about 500 percent and shared a spumoni as they drank their coffee.

Jo said it was so difficult to begin a relationship when there were so many expectations. What she asked of Curt and promised of herself was to have none, no expectations! Like the boat Curt lived on, *The Drifter*, let them see where the seas of life would take them. Curt really loved that and agreed.

After dinner, he asked if he could drive her home and see her apartment. He'd seen the outside when he picked her up that day to visit City Island, but he really wanted to see how she lived. Curt felt you could tell a lot about a person by their home. Jo said, "Of course," and had a pretty good idea as to where this would lead them. She longed for him so and felt his unspoken desire as well.

They held hands and were silent as they walked to Curt's car. Jo remembered that so vividly. A smile and a tear came to her face, and for a moment, in that bar (as she was reflecting on the past), she wished she could go back in time to when their true, eternal love began.

As expected, at Jo's apartment, they made love the entire night—not the lustful, ravaging explosion of lust they'd experienced on *The Drifter*, but soulful, beyond a mere intimate bonding of two beings. It was the likes of which she had never felt before.

In the morning, she called in to her office and asked for a "well-being day" and, with her boss's approval, reveled in the joy of spending the entire day with Curt. They never got dressed. What a sight they must have been to anyone else, but to each other, they were beautiful. After all, if you were only going to take meal breaks in between lovemaking, what was the point of taking clothes on and off all day?

By dinnertime, they truly needed a physical break and, almost demurely, took separate showers and dressed. Jo lived in a wonderful neighborhood and sent Curt out for dinner at the nearby grocer. She insisted on paying for the food; after all, he had paid for dinner the night before. He yielded with a smile because they had just committed to a real partnership.

Jo recalled with absolute delight that she never really had this kind of "normal" feeling in any of her past relationships. Short of her ex-husband, who was less than passionate with her, every other man had been an affair. No matter what you called them, that's what they all were. As far as she was concerned, this looked like it could be the beginning of something big (as corny as that sounded).

Jo remembered that evening so well. It had been a line in the sand for her, the beginning of the rest of her life, so she thought.

The recollection was almost frightening to her. *How can you remember so much, in such detail, when it was so many years ago?* She came to the conclusion at this bar on this afternoon that some things were just meant to be etched in her heart forever. She ordered another glass of merlot. It would be her final one, forever, in The Club.

The love affair with Curt fell into a very comfortable, unpredictable pattern. They both liked it very much. Curt continued to live on *The Drifter*, and Jo was very happy in her little apartment in Brooklyn. Curt began his first long-haul truck trip and, just like he'd predicted, was gone from New York for almost a month. They spoke every day, and Jo felt very connected even though Curt had ended up in California and was working his way back. Jo was so pleased he was safe and looked forward to his return. She occupied her days with work; her nights and weekends were filled with friends. She couldn't wait to introduce them to her man.

Curt's first night back was to be a celebration, Jo remembered. She left work early, stopped at the wine store for a lovely bottle of 2006 Côte-Rôtie Brune et Blonde from the Rhône region of France that the wine master said would be superb with the strip steaks she was going to buy next along with salad fixings, baking potatoes, and a homemade peach-and-raspberry cobbler from the bakery near where she lived. She wanted to spoil the heck out of Curt and revel in his first long-haul job.

Curt arrived with flowers, filling Jo's little apartment with the sweet scents of a florist shop. It was glorious. Their kiss was so long they both were afraid they'd pass out from the joy. When they came up for air, they roared with laughter and wondered if it were just lust and would pass or if they had truly found each other's soul mates.

Curt helped with the salad as Jo cooked the steaks on her tiny indoor grill. They lit candles, put on some soft James Taylor, poured wine, and ate with as much delight as if they'd been together forever.

Although they'd talked daily while Curt was gone, Jo wanted a day-by-day history of his first long-haul adventure. Curt wanted to hear everything from her as well, and thus began a true give-and-take relationship in this blossoming new event called true love. She actually listened to how he really didn't like stopping at truck stops and sleeping in the back of the cab, but he'd done a good job: he had made all his deadlines and was free until the next order came through.

He was happy to be back on *The Drifter* and missed Jo beyond words. Then came her turn. "Same old, same old," she said. Work was good; she'd gone to see a play with some girlfriends, walked around Central Park one Saturday, read her book, got a haircut, got her by-weekly manicure and pedicure, and "that was about that." They both laughed out loud because they already knew all of everything since they'd spoken every day since Curt had gone. *What fun,* Jo remembered. *A really, really nice man.*

Jo was so pleased that Curt helped her clean up. The two then sat in her small living room and had an after-dinner aperitif. She never felt more at home, and she was home with the most special man she had ever met. *Why?* Jo asked herself. She gave it some quiet thought and then realized he was just a good guy. She loved that.

They were just like a pair of deliciously broken-in old shoes that made you feel so comfortable just wearing them.

Curt broke the silence and asked her if she wanted to make love. No one had ever asked her that before, it had just always been assumed. She couldn't resist saying yes.

He took her that night to places she'd never been before. She had no idea such rapture was even possible. His joy in her joy sent him into a mad desire, and he took her with all the tenderness he possessed. Over and over, they stroked each other and kissed each other and intertwined with each other. Jo had never felt this way before. She thought Curt had unleashed a part of her being she never knew existed.

After her less-than-fulfilling sexual experience with her husband, she'd always held herself back completely for fear of being hurt again. With Curt, she wanted to go to places she never dreamed were possible.

Finally, they stopped, and as Curt dressed, Jo thought, *I could be with this man forever.*

Thus began the memory of memories.

The Next Ten Years (Almost)

As they began a true, loving relationship, Jo got used to Curt having to leave for long hauls. It was good for them to have these breaks; Jo got to see her friends, and Curt strived for a deadline and was consumed with his work when he was gone. When he was home, they were inseparable. She loved it. The time came, after a while, for each of them to meet each other's friends. Jo had many; Curt really only had one—the man who owned *The Drifter*. His name was Sam, and he was very private. He had met Curt, so he told Jo, when he was wandering around New York. They were as different as night and day—Sam and Curt—but they still took a great liking to each other. Jo accepted this story, she recalled. It seemed a little bizarre, but given her life, who was she to question anyone? Sam was pleased to meet Jo, and he invited them to his apartment on Fifth Avenue in the city for dinner the following Saturday night.

Jo remembered being excited to meet the man who allowed *The Drifter* to be Curt's home. As she dressed for her very important date, she pondered as to what the appropriate wear should be. She certainly didn't want to appear in any way too sexy. A woman of her age walked a fine line between sexy and smart. *Smart* was the operative word here, and she chose a simple Diane von Furstenberg wrap dress. Although it showed her figure to be in great shape, she felt it was just the right thing to wear. Curt had given her a heads-up that Sam was somewhat eccentric, but fun. Jo was very excited to meet this significant man in Curt's life and was up for anything.

Curt arrived to pick her up wearing a sport shirt, jacket, and khaki pants. He looked gorgeous, and Jo remembered having to control her desire. Funny thing is, in all their years together, she *never* lost her desire for him, nor he for her.

They got to Sam's at seven that evening. The doorman valeted the car, and they took an elevator directly to the penthouse. Jo was speechless. How did Curt and this very wealthy man become connected? It was a true puzzle that she was anxious to unravel.

Sam met them at the door with a warm smile and open arms. She instantly felt welcomed. To cut to the chase, they all had a glorious evening together. Sam told of how he and Curt had met through a mutual friend many years ago, and when Curt decided to return to New York, Sam offered *The Drifter* to Curt as his home. Sam said Curt was actually doing him a favor by watching the boat as Sam traveled a great deal and was pleased to have Curt living there. The trucking stuff was not a problem as Sam had arranged for the dock master to have the boat watched when Curt was on the road. Sam and the dock master had become very close friends over the years. All seemed to make sense at the time.

Sam reveled in hearing about Jo and how she and Curt had met. All in all, it was an evening to remember. At an appropriate time, they thanked Sam for his hospitality and said they looked forward to seeing him again. Sam insisted they come for Sunday dinner any week they were free. They said they would, hugged in a friendly embrace, and headed for the car and Jo's apartment. Jo couldn't remember how so many of these memories were so vivid and deeply etched in her mind.

Jo had asked Curt to spend the night if he wanted to, knowing quite well she had to work tomorrow. Curt smiled and said with a naughty chuckle, "Are you kidding?"

The night that followed took her breath away. How could a man evoke such passion out of her? She had to stop thinking for a moment as she sat at the bar at The Club. As long ago as that had been, the feelings still were raw, powerful, and otherworldly.

Their lovemaking continued like this every time they were together. Jo remembered how they fell into a very comfortable pattern when they were with one another. She recalled how unusual it was that they had kept separate residences throughout their entire love affair. And that's what it had been—a true, honest-to-goodness love affair. Neither one of them saw any reason to move in together.

Curt loved *The Drifter*, and Jo needed to be closer to the city for work and loved her little nest as well. The distance between them, along with Curt's travels, made their reunions feel like a new beginning every time they met. *Perhaps,* Jo thought, *this was the magic of our love.* Neither took any part of their relationship for granted, and they both had such respect for each other.

Over time, Jo introduced Curt to all her friends, and from time to time, they socialized. Most Sundays that Curt was not on the road, they dined with Sam, who soon became very close to Jo over the years. It was evident that the life Curt and she had created for themselves was perfect. Neither wanted anything more from the other, and that allowed for true self-expression and freedom.

As dusk began to fall, Jo realized it was time to leave The Club.

Perhaps she'd end this adventure tomorrow afternoon, and what had started out to be one afternoon was now turning into three. She had many more memories to go; perhaps tomorrow would be the day her adventure ended.

The third day of this little afternoon adventure was bittersweet. Her work went well, as usual. She took a cab over to The Club around two o'clock. She had skipped lunch so she could have time to once again reflect on Curt and all the joy he had brought her.

As she sauntered up to her old barstool, she took an envelope from her purse and laid it on the bar. First things first: a hearty sandwich and a glass of wine. Her head started to spin; she'd not had lunch, and it had been a long time since breakfast. She had to steady herself. The rest of the day might become overwhelming to her. She thought of work as she ate. Jo wanted a clear head when she recounted the end of her time with Curt.

After her late lunch, she decided to move downstairs to the restaurant part of the bar and take a small table in a quiet corner for fear she might get emotional as she recalled their ending. The music was low, and so were the lights. To her, it was the perfect spot to conclude the afternoon, no matter how long it took to complete. She appreciated Frank Sinatra quietly singing his love songs, as always, in the background.

There was no doubt; her life with Curt had been an extraordinary experience. They had almost ten years of "unwedded bliss." She was fortunate to still have her job, and Curt was happy, all those years, to be on the road. Their breaks left them so appreciative of their reunions. Jo never realized there could be such a sustaining, unrequited love.

Sam became the third member of their unconventional family dynamic. He brought everything to the party that money could buy. Jo thought he might have been close to seventy-five years when they first met, but it was very hard to tell peoples' ages these days for Jo. Sam was so generous and, over the years, sent them to Europe, the Caribbean, and the Orient. At first, they outright declined his offers but succumbed when he told them that they had become his family too and it was his joy to share his good fortune and wealth. After all, they were the closest thing to a real family that he had.

Sam came along on several of these trips when he didn't have much to do. He never interfered with their time together, though. This was a pattern for nearly ten years: a trip a year to some delicious part of the world with the man she loved. It was beyond her wildest dreams.

The End

Aside from not having rings and vows and living in the same physical location, Jo and Curt had the best relationship she had ever experienced. Many of her friends were married, and most of them bitched about their husbands constantly. Jo learned early on that sometimes people don't want to hear about your happiness, especially when they are moaning about their lives. She learned to be very low-key about Curt, and although they all knew him and liked him; none of them knew the extent of the passion in their relationship. She felt it was best to keep it private.

It was during one winter, as she recalled, and the weather had been especially brutal in New York. Jo remembered being so worried every time Curt left the terminal with a load going out west, but he constantly returned to her safe and sound, and they had always picked up with each other right where they left off, as if they had only left each other's sides for a few moments.

Both of them had passed their sixty-fifth birthday, and both were overwhelmed as to how two very middle-aged people could sustain such a love affair. It always felt new, yet as comfortable as forever. They truly felt like the luckiest people on earth. It was so simple to be this happy, content, and deeply in love. She often wondered why so many people could not find this kind of happiness. She concluded, "Too many expectations!"

Jo looked at the envelope on the small table at The Club, and tears streaked down her cheeks. New tears, but they had been there many times before. She ordered her last glass of wine at The Club and continued playing out the memory in her head.

Years had gone by, and aside from an occasional cold, both she and Curt were in reasonably good health for their ages. Curt made a point of working out as much as he could and "run" around truck stops when he was on the road. She was not as diligent as he, but she walked all over New York daily and surely felt that that counted as exercise. Every now and then, she would accompany a girlfriend to a class at the gym. She was making no excuses, but she held her own with Curt—just in a different way. They both felt good about themselves. Life was great.

They always made a big deal of Christmas with Sam since it seemed the three of them were family. One year, Sam took them to Paris to celebrate the New Year. There was nothing in her memory that compared with snow falling down over the Eiffel Tower, twinkling with a million lights, and fireworks going off and drinking champagne at a nearby bistro with a direct view of it all.

And then came the end.

It was early spring, and the flowers were attempting to stick their glorious heads above what was left of the snow in the city. Curt and Jo had had a wild night of passionate love, as they always did before he embarked on a long trip. This was so old hat to them, yet so new . . . it always felt as though it might be their last. They both knew there were risks of being on the roads, but to tell the truth, Jo never let herself go there in her mind. After all, Curt had a stellar driving record; he was a master trucker, if there was such a term.

Curt left for the West Coast with many stops along the way. They talked every night when Curt stopped for the day. Truckers are federally regulated as to how many hours they can drive each twenty-four-hour period. Jo, being left behind, fell into her pattern of girly things to do with her gal pals. She also had decided, with Sam's prodding and Curt's encouragement, to spend Sundays with Sam. He was much older, of course, but he kept up with her as they visited museums and art galleries and had glorious dinners both out and in his magnificent penthouse. He had live-in help and a cook. She never worried about him. There was a staff of three to look after him. After all, if one was in good health, the early eighties was not the end of the road for anyone. Besides, if he'd ever really gotten sick, he would have the very best medical care possible.

Her mind wandered back to her darling Curt. For years they'd shared their day-to-day lives when apart and *lived* their day-to-day lives when they were together. For both of them, it was the best life imaginable.

One day, Sam called Jo while Curt was on one of his long hauls and asked if Jo could come over for dinner. It was during the week, and Jo hesitated. She had work, obviously, but she said yes as long as Sam realized she would leave early. It was to be a little different. She called Curt's cell phone and got his voice mail. She told him to reach her at Sam's that evening. It was unusual for Sam to even call her midweek, but she concluded he must have just been lonesome or something.

She cabbed to Fifth Avenue, and the doorman welcomed her, as he had done for years when she and Curt would dine with Sam.

Sam greeted her at the door himself just like the first time they'd met so many years ago. Usually, the maid answered the door. Jo thought this was somewhat strange, but Sam was slightly eccentric, as she learned way back then. He hugged her especially long and hard that night; he kissed her cheek and asked her to join him in his library for a "before dinner" drink. She had grown so fond of Sam over the years and truly felt that he had somewhat made up for her parents, who were many years gone.

The maid brought them some freshly baked nibbles as Sam poured them each a Johnnie Walker Blue on the rocks. Jo had a horrible distaste for hard liquor but didn't want to disrespect Sam's hospitality. They settled into Sam's deep-burgundy leather chairs to enjoy their time before dinner. But Jo knew that something was wrong. They had done this so many times before—Curt, Sam, and Jo—but something was certainly off tonight. *This memory feels so vivid,* thought Jo.

Sam was uncomfortable with their small talk and, somewhat like Curt, said, "Jo, I have something to tell you, and before I do, I want you to know that I will always be here for you."

She was perplexed. "What is it Sam? Please?"

Sam took a sip of his scotch, sat down next to Jo, took her hand, and said very quietly, "Curt is . . . gone. He's dead."

Jo's breath was suspended as she let out a wail beyond grief. Sam held her as she cried and cried and cried. Sometimes she screamed between tears, and Sam never let her go as she went through the shock of it all. About an hour went by, and Jo finally looked at Sam and saw the tears running down his cheeks as well. She pulled back and, in utter disbelief, was able to get a few words out before crying once more. Her scotch glass was on the floor; Sam didn't care, and Jo was in shock.

"Sam, what happened? Where is he? Why did you know before I did?" They unlocked arms, consumed a box of Kleenex, and Sam did his best, through his own tears, to tell her everything.

At The Club, as Jo was reliving this unbelievable event, her tears were so apparent that the server came over to ask if she needed anything. Jo said, "No, thank you, just let me be, please." The woman walked away quietly to leave Jo with her memories.

Sam said Curt was on a very steep incline on Interstate 70, just above Glenwood Springs, on his way to drop a large load in Vail, Colorado. It had snowed lightly the night before, and then the sun had come out, making it appear the roads were safe. But there was still a very thin layer of ice on the incline. Curt came through that part of the road about seven o'clock at night, and the ice was just setting up. It was just a fluke. Curt's trailer swerved a little, according to the tire tracks, the police had said, and it was just enough to make Curt's cab spin and turn over into the ditch. He hit two trees while going over, and they think he was killed instantly as one of the trees had come through the windshield on the driver's side.

Jo remembered screaming, wailing, and crying forever, it seemed, in Sam's arms. He was openly crying again himself.

When they both came up for air, Jo had some more scotch and once again asked the question, "How did you know before I did, Sam?" After all, Sam was just a friend, and Jo was Curt's love, soul mate, partner, and everything else. Sam said this was the time to tell her why.

Sam really was Curt's father. Jo remembered thinking she was going to pass out, but she composed herself long enough to listen to Sam tell the story. Sam picked up the phone and asked the maid to bring two trays of something light to eat; they might be staying in the library for quite a while and would not be dining in the big room tonight. Sam and Jo sat, silently weeping, and the maid entered and departed with nary a sound. She knew of Curt's death, as did all the staff, and, out of respect, said nothing.

Jo remembered sitting in disbelief. All of this was more than she could fathom; it was too overwhelming. First, Sam being Curt's father, and then Curt's death. It was truly out of a bad dream. Jo was quiet enough at the moment to ask Sam why Curt never told her about his father.

Sam gave her a hug and asked her if she was up to hearing the bizarre story of his life with Curt. She said yes, and they both agreed that tears over the loss of Curt might come up at any time, and they both agreed this was to be expected and was OK with them. They would hold back no grief.

Sam assured her that if it were too much for Jo at any time, Sam would stop. Somehow they managed to eat a little tomato bisque and fresh sourdough bread as Sam explained. Sam poured more scotch for the both of them.

Curt had had such a different childhood from Jo's, which led her to truly believe in the saying "Opposites attract." Curt's parents had never been married in the first place, so when he was born, his mother was already a single parent. They lived in New York City, and on a good day, if you didn't have a great deal of money, you were already behind the eight ball, so to speak. Curt's mother did her best to provide for her only child, but day care took most of her weekly paycheck.

This went on for several years until his mother found a way to make a substantial amount of money. Curt was too young to know why his mother went out almost every night, but she always left him with reliable child sitters. They lived in Brooklyn by this time, and it was a very short cab ride into the city to service her clients.

Jo didn't even know the details of it all; it must have been so painful for Curt when he was old enough to learn that his mother had been an escort.

At some point, Curt had completely blocked it all out—which was why he was so surprised when child services visited their apartment and took him away. He was devastated; after all, his mother was his rock even though she chose to live a very unconventional life. Curt was five and had just started kindergarten. The loss of his mother was more than he could comprehend.

A lovely foster family provided him a good home for many years, but the mother didn't possess the nurturing he longed for from his own mother, and his rebellion and anger had been so strong that, after about nine years, they could no longer handle Curt and gave him back to the State. At fourteen, it was very unlikely that anyone would want him, so he lived in an orphanage until the day Sam came into his life. Of course, Curt never told Jo any of this.

Sam was an enigma, a not-yet-middle-aged man of great wealth. Sam had never married: that was the first puzzle. At about age thirty-five, Sam, a very rich and lonely man, decided to adopt a boy who needed a very good home. Having a stable home of privilege, Sam had no trouble qualifying for a child. He chose Curt, who had been in foster care for many years. Sam saw so many qualities in Curt and a great potential. It seemed that all he needed was a loving, nurturing home, and Sam could surely provide that for him. Curt was about fifteen at the time and liked Sam very much. It was a wonderful life. Curt had everything any teenage boy could ask for. Sam put Curt in a private school in the city and delighted at how well Curt adapted.

He was an excellent student and, after high school, attended Brown University, where he majored in business with the idea of joining Sam in his international endeavors after graduation. By twenty-two, Curt told Sam that although he was so appreciative of all that Sam had provided for him, he wanted to try different things. Sam was devastated, as should be expected, but he told Curt that he would support him in whatever future he had planned for himself. He just hoped that no matter where Curt went, they would always stay connected. Curt agreed and began drifting all over the world, like the vagabond Jo remembered from the story Sam told.

Curt lived in Europe for many years and then New Orleans, where he was a fisherman. He sold insurance for a short time, as he had told Jo. At some point, around ten years ago, he decided to move back to Manhattan. Curt did not want to live in Sam's palatial penthouse on Fifth Avenue and compromised when Sam offered him *The Drifter*. Curt agreed, with much gratitude, and moved it, with Sam's permission, from the New York City Yacht Club to City Island. It suited him better, he said.

Then Jo had entered his life, and the rest of the tale Jo could recite moment by moment. By the time Sam ended, Jo was spent, so overcome with grief she could take no more. Sam asked her to spend the night so they'd continue in the morning. Jo remembered being so grateful that she wouldn't have to go home with her grief just yet. One of the maids brought her to one of the many guest rooms, and Jo remembered collapsing onto the bed and just crying herself to sleep.

The tears hurt her heart. She couldn't believe that Curt, the true love of her life, was gone forever. Somehow, though, she finally fell asleep in her deep sadness. In the morning, she washed up and dressed mechanically, trying to conserve what little strength she had to meet Sam downstairs.

Breakfast was set up on the sideboard in the dining room, and once Jo saw Sam, she ran to him and hugged him, her eyes flooded with tears. She only wanted coffee, and Sam gently nudged her to at least have a little fruit and eggs. She took the food to be polite but could hardly get it down.

Tears rolled down Jo's face as she recollected this moment with Sam.

By now, The Club was beginning to fill up with the after-work crowd making their happy-hour pit stop before heading for home.

It had been two years since Curt's passing, and it was still hard not to miss his huge laugh and grin, especially right before he kissed her. She didn't know if she could ever get over the loss of the greatest love she had ever known.

Jo remembered, so vividly, asking Sam what was to become of Curt, and he said the Colorado police were making arrangements to have his body shipped back to New York. Since there were no other people involved in the accident, an autopsy was not necessary. The police had directed Sam to a very reputable funeral home in Vail, which would prepare Curt for his return to New York. Jo began crying again. There was so much pent-up shock and denial in her she wasn't sure she could ever get past it.

Sam was an amazing rock for her. He had come to love her as his own, as he had Curt so many years ago. Sam called Jo's boss and asked for a bereavement leave, then asked her to stay with him. He sent his housekeeper to Brooklyn to gather her personal necessities and clothes.

For days, as they waited for Curt to arrive back in New York, Jo and Sam spent hours crying and sharing stories of Curt. Neither of them could accept the tragedy. Sam's business manager made all the arrangements for Curt's remains to be cremated in New York, and then Jo and Sam decided to hold a special ceremony to celebrate Curt's life.

After about a week, Curt arrived back in New York, and Jo wanted to see him before he became ashes. Sam's driver took them to the funeral home, and after Sam said a lengthy farewell, Jo entered the room where Curt's body was encased in a casket made of pine, ready for the fire. The funeral director said the box was sealed and she couldn't see him, but she knew he was there with her.

Jo needed another glass of wine at The Club as she recalled the end of her love affairs. She ordered something light to eat for fear she'd get drunk on an empty stomach. Funny, she thought, as she remembered these moments, she almost had a smile on her face, just reveling in the gloriousness of Curt despite as devastating as the end had been.

In that room at the funeral home, alone with Curt, she whispered to him how much she loved him and how he had filled her life with unbridled joy for so many years and how she hoped she had given him as much. She also told him how mad she was with him for being dead, for leaving her alone without him. After the ceremony, Jo and Sam left the funeral home, consoling each other as best they could.

Sam asked Jo what she would like to do with Curt's ashes, and she said there was only one thing to do—but only if it was OK with Sam. He agreed.

Curt arrived in a gorgeous urn two days later, and once again, Jo and Sam cried. Jo hugged the urn and wailed as if her heart would truly break at that moment. They had made arrangements for the dock master to meet them at *The Drifter*, and as Sam and Jo drove to City Island with the urn between them, the silence was deafening. Sam's driver let them out at the dock and waited for them. Jo carried the urn to the boat, and the dock master helped Sam down the pier.. He helped them both board *The Drifter*, and he started the engine as they seated themselves and let the wind soothe them.

It was a cold day, very unlike Jo's first afternoon on the boat. They cruised very slowly out into the harbor, and finally, about three miles out, Jo said, "Stop. This is the place for Curt." The dock master helped Jo open the urn, and Sam let some of the ashes hit the sea. He cried as he said farewell to the best son a man could ask for. Then he went below so Jo could say good-bye to Curt in private. As she scattered his remains into the sea, she professed her love again and recited e. e. Cummings's "I Carry You in My Heart." When all the ashes were gone, she let a dozen white roses float in the sea and follow Curt to heaven.

On the way back to the city, Sam told her he had something for her from Curt. She was in disbelief. She had been staying with Sam for a few days, so why would he be giving her something from Curt now? Sam could see the shock on her face, and he said Curt had asked him not to give this to Jo until the right time. "Today is the right time," Sam said. When they returned to the city, Sam gave her the envelope Curt had left for her.

It was the same envelope Jo had with her in The Club that afternoon.

Sam poured Jo a glass of wine and left her to be alone with Curt in that envelope. Jo thanked him and hugged and kissed him. She opened the envelope carefully with a gilded letter opener that was on Sam's desk. This was so sacred to her, and she didn't want to deface even the envelope. It said, "To Jo—the one and only true love of my life."

Jo pulled out a two-page, handwritten letter from Curt to her. She had to stop crying before she could begin reading it because her tears blurred her vision. She gave herself permission to cry until she didn't need to cry anymore, and then she began to read.

The first sentence startled her back into reality.

Dearest Jo,

Love of my life, if you are reading this letter, then I am no longer with you. I am dead.

I asked Sam, my wonderful father, to hold this for me until it was the right time to give it to you. This must be the right time. I trust him.

I began to write this letter to you on my first cross-country road trip, not knowing what would happen. No matter how brave a man pretends to be, we are as scared of the unknown as women. We just don't let it out. We had just met, you and I, and our lust and passion had been so overwhelming, I wasn't sure if it was something real or just my desire for a woman to want me for me. That's the reason I chose not to tell you about my life with Sam. Sam understood as so many women in the past had been taken with Sam's wealth and, therefore, thought they could get to him through me.

Enough of this prelude stuff. Jo, I fell in love with you so quickly it terrified me. Of course, I couldn't tell you: I didn't want to frighten you away.

Jo smiled through her tears as she read the letter; she had been so afraid of scaring Curt away if she had professed her love for him early. Funny how totally compatible they truly were.

Curt continued.

As I fell more madly in love with you, I truly knew I'd finally found the woman of my dreams. Your funny laugh, your generous heart, your unabashed passion, of which I'd never known so intently, fulfilled my life. I was so frightened it would pass, but you, Jo, the remarkable love of my life, never changed. All these years, you gave me everything.

Jo was crying so hard now that she had to put the letter down and just let the grief out. She cried for hours as she remembered. Then she dialed the maid, from Sam's library, and asked for a cup of chamomile tea and, after a few calming sips, continued to read.

Jo, there is nothing I can do to ease your pain. If I were there holding you and comforting you, this letter would serve no purpose. I hoped this day would never come. I prayed we'd grow older and comfort each other in our old age. I no longer have that, but I intend to watch over and protect you as you go forth in your life.

You need to know there was never anyone in my life that I loved more than you. You were and now are my angel on earth. Sam will always be there for you, and I have left something with him for you.

Good-bye, my darling, my sweet, my love, my everything. I will love you from heaven forever.

With all the love I have to give, I want you to know you will be with me for eternity.

Love, Curt.

Jo put the letter down, and a remarkable sense of peace came over her. She called for Sam and politely let him know that she would like to return to her little place in Brooklyn to be alone. Sam said, "Of course," and sent for his car to take her home. He would have his maid gather her things in the morning and have them delivered. She begged Sam not to call her. She would be back in touch with him when the time was right. He said he completely understood.

Jo cried silently all the way to Brooklyn in the back of the limousine. The driver, who'd been with Sam for years, knew enough to let her be. She thanked him when they arrived and was so grateful to be home. She immediately closed the shades, got into her pajamas, and tucked herself into bed. Once again, she cried herself to sleep. Jo didn't even know what day it was when she woke up. After a call to her office requesting an extended vacation, Jo made some tea and returned to bed.

After several days, she awoke to a feeling of selfishness. *What about Sam? He's obviously grieving too.* Jo called to see how he was doing and discovered that, like her, he had been very reclusive since Curt's death. Sam asked Jo if she was up for dinner on Sunday, like they used to have, the three of them, for so many years. Jo said she'd like that, and ever since that first Sunday dinner after Curt's death, they dined every single week on Sunday in honor of Curt. Sam gave her a box from Curt containing a diamond angel pendant and a large insurance policy that Curt had taken out with Jo as its beneficiary. She remembered being very reluctant to take it, but Sam insisted that Curt had set this up almost nine years ago and wanted Jo to have it.

It had been almost two years since Curt's death, and as Jo sat in the corner at The Club, she took out the letter one more time and read it slowly. Tears gently streamed down her face as she recalled, once more, their years together. She almost felt his presence but knew this was just a longing for him. She finished the letter and her glass of wine, put on her coat, and said good-bye to The Club for the last time.

As she walked toward the front door, so many memories of her good old days came rushing back. She smiled. This club seemed to hold a life she no longer needed or wanted. Jo truly felt that her love for Curt fulfilled everything she could have ever wanted and, in retrospect, more than she ever expected in her life. Her life was far from over, but there would never be a love waiting for her greater than Curt.

She had started this adventure three afternoons ago; having no idea it would take so many days to come full circle. Jo had begun her quest to see if she still had *it*. She now thought how preposterous a question that was. She did have it—she'd had it all. No woman could have asked for more.

The End

Edwards Brothers Malloy
Thorofare, NJ USA
May 21, 2013